Mum Bug has a red bag.
The bag has a zip.

1

Mum can fit a pen in her bag.

2

Mum can fit a pen and
a fan in her bag.

Mum can fit a pen and
a fan and
a bun in her bag.

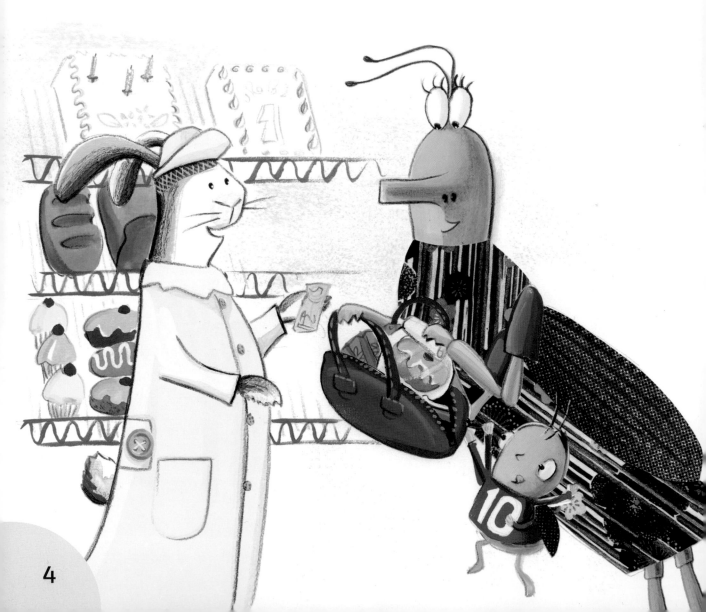

Mum can fit a pen and
a fan and
a bun and
a pot of jam in her bag.

Mum has a hole in her bag!

The pen and
the fan and
the bun and
the jam get wet.

Mum Bug gets a big bag.